Dear Parents:

Congratulations! Your child is taking the first steps on an exciting journey. The destination? Independent reading!

STEP INTO READING® will help your child get there. The program offers five steps to reading success. Each step includes fun stories and colorful art or photographs. In addition to original fiction and books with favorite characters, there are Step into Reading Non-Fiction Readers, Phonics Readers and Boxed Sets, Sticker Readers, and Comic Readers—a complete literacy program with something to interest every child.

Learning to Read, Step by Step!

Ready to Read   Preschool–Kindergarten
• big type and easy words • rhyme and rhythm • picture clues
For children who know the alphabet and are eager to begin reading.

Reading with Help   Preschool–Grade 1
• basic vocabulary • short sentences • simple stories
For children who recognize familiar words and sound out new words with help.

Reading on Your Own   Grades 1–3
• engaging characters • easy-to-follow plots • popular topics
For children who are ready to read on their own.

Reading Paragraphs   Grades 2–3
• challenging vocabulary • short paragraphs • exciting stories
For newly independent readers who read simple sentences with confidence.

Ready for Chapters   Grades 2–4
• chapters • longer paragraphs • full-color art
For children who want to take the plunge into chapter books but still like colorful pictures.

STEP INTO READING® is designed to give every child a successful reading experience. The grade levels are only guides; children will progress through the steps at their own speed, developing confidence in their reading.

Remember, a lifetime love of reading starts with a single step!

For wonder women everywhere,
may you always fly as high and far
as you possibly can.
—C.B.C.

All rights reserved. Published in the United States by Random House Children's Books, a division
of Penguin Random House LLC, 1745 Broadway, New York, NY 10019, and in Canada by
Random House of Canada, a division of Penguin Random House Ltd., Toronto.

Step into Reading, Random House, and the Random House colophon are registered trademarks
of Penguin Random House LLC.

Visit us on the Web!
StepIntoReading.com
randomhousekids.com
dckids.kidswb.com

Educators and librarians, for a variety of teaching tools, visit us at RHTeachersLibrarians.com

ISBN 978-1-101-93308-4 (trade)
ISBN 978-1-101-93309-1 (lib. bdg.)
ISBN 978-1-101-93310-7 (ebook)

Printed in the United States of America
10 9 8 7 6 5 4 3 2

STEP 2 READING WITH HELP

STEP INTO READING®

DC SUPER FRIENDS™

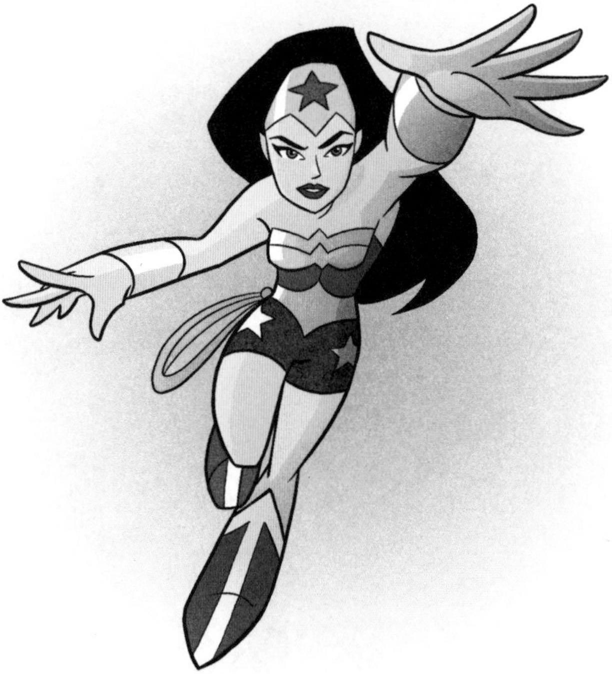

WONDER WOMAN TO THE RESCUE!

by Courtney Carbone

illustrated by Erik Doescher

Wonder Woman created
by William Moulton Marston

Random House New York

Meet Wonder Woman!

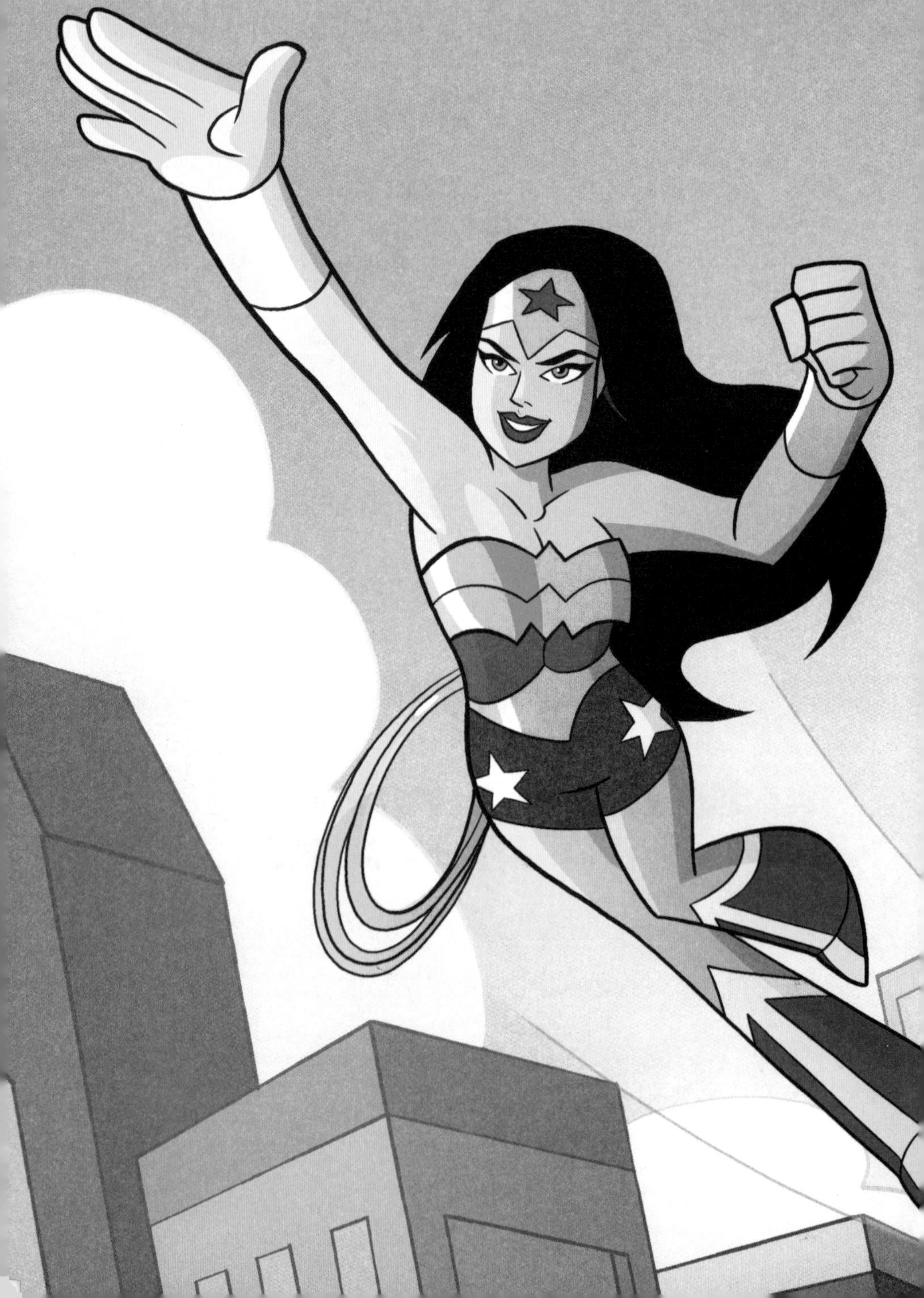

She is a super hero
and a warrior princess.

Wonder Woman grew up
on Paradise Island.

Her mother was queen
of the Amazons.

The Greek gods gave Wonder Woman power to fight evil on Earth.

She uses the name
Diana Prince
as her secret identity.

Wonder Woman has
a tiara with a red star.
It can be used
as a weapon!

Wonder Woman has
shiny metal bracelets.
They cannot be broken!

Wonder Woman also has
a Golden Lasso of Truth!

The lasso makes
bad guys tell the truth.

Wonder Woman has
many special skills.
She is smart, strong,
fast, and brave!

She is also a master
of combat.

Smash! Crash! Bash!

Wonder Woman flies
an Invisible Jet.

Here she comes

to save the day!

Wonder Woman
stops Cheetah
in her tracks!

Cheetah cannot keep
her claws out
of trouble.

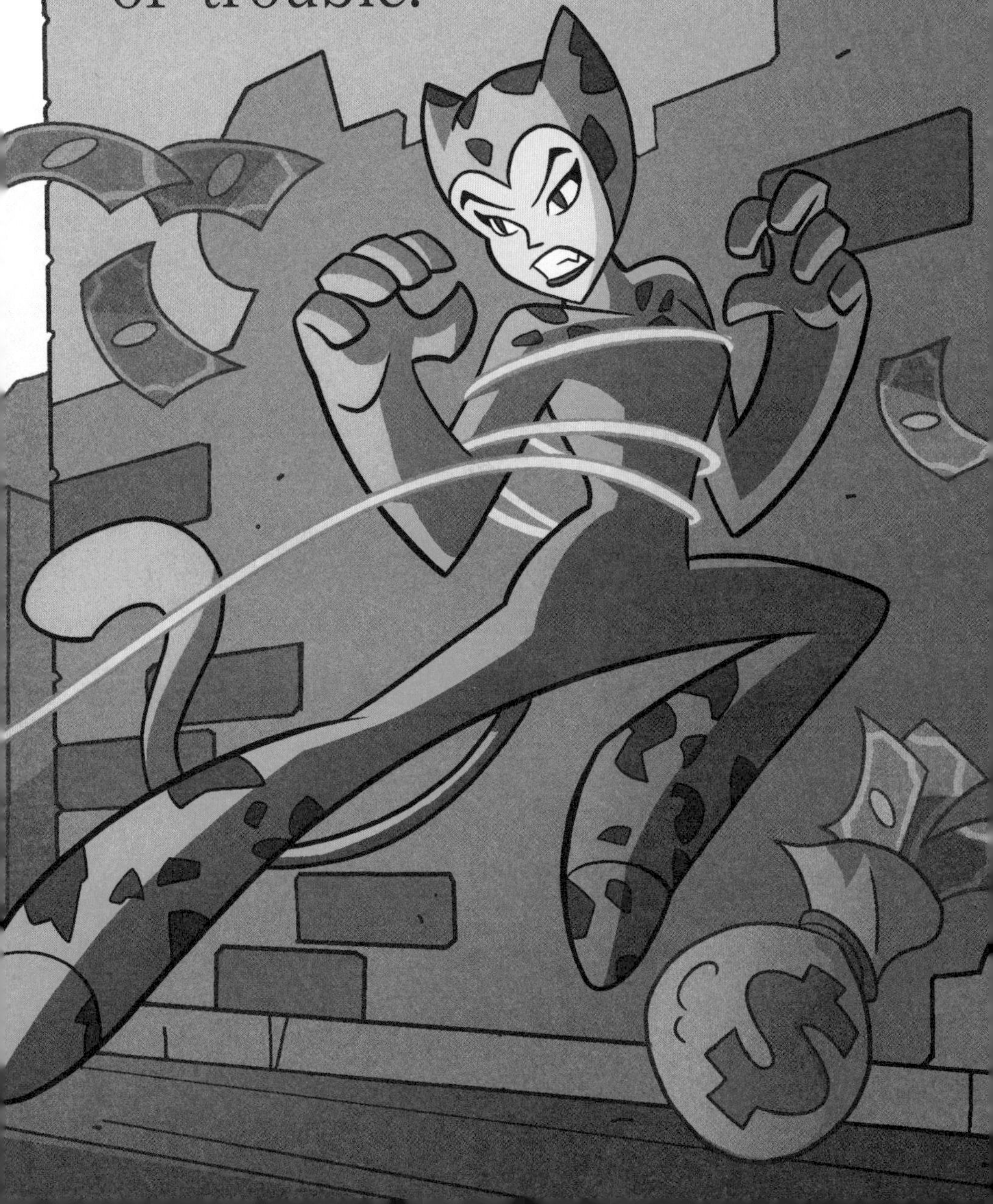

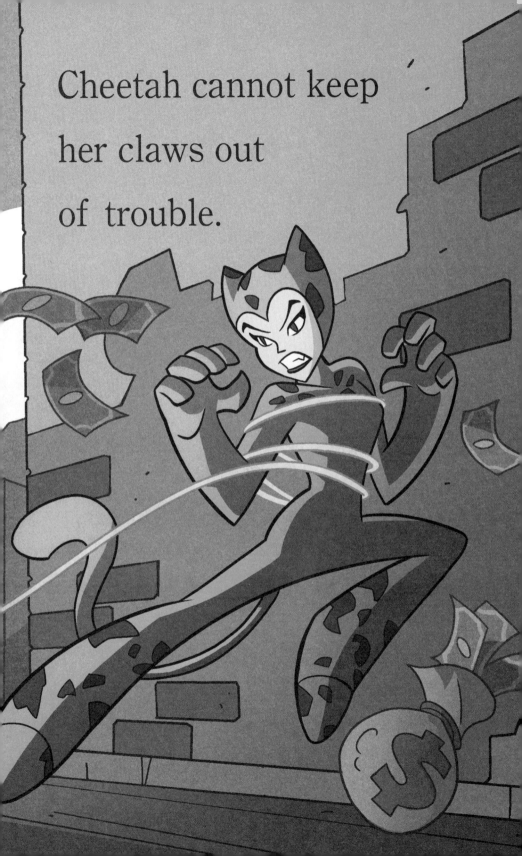

Wonder Woman has
lots of Super Friends.

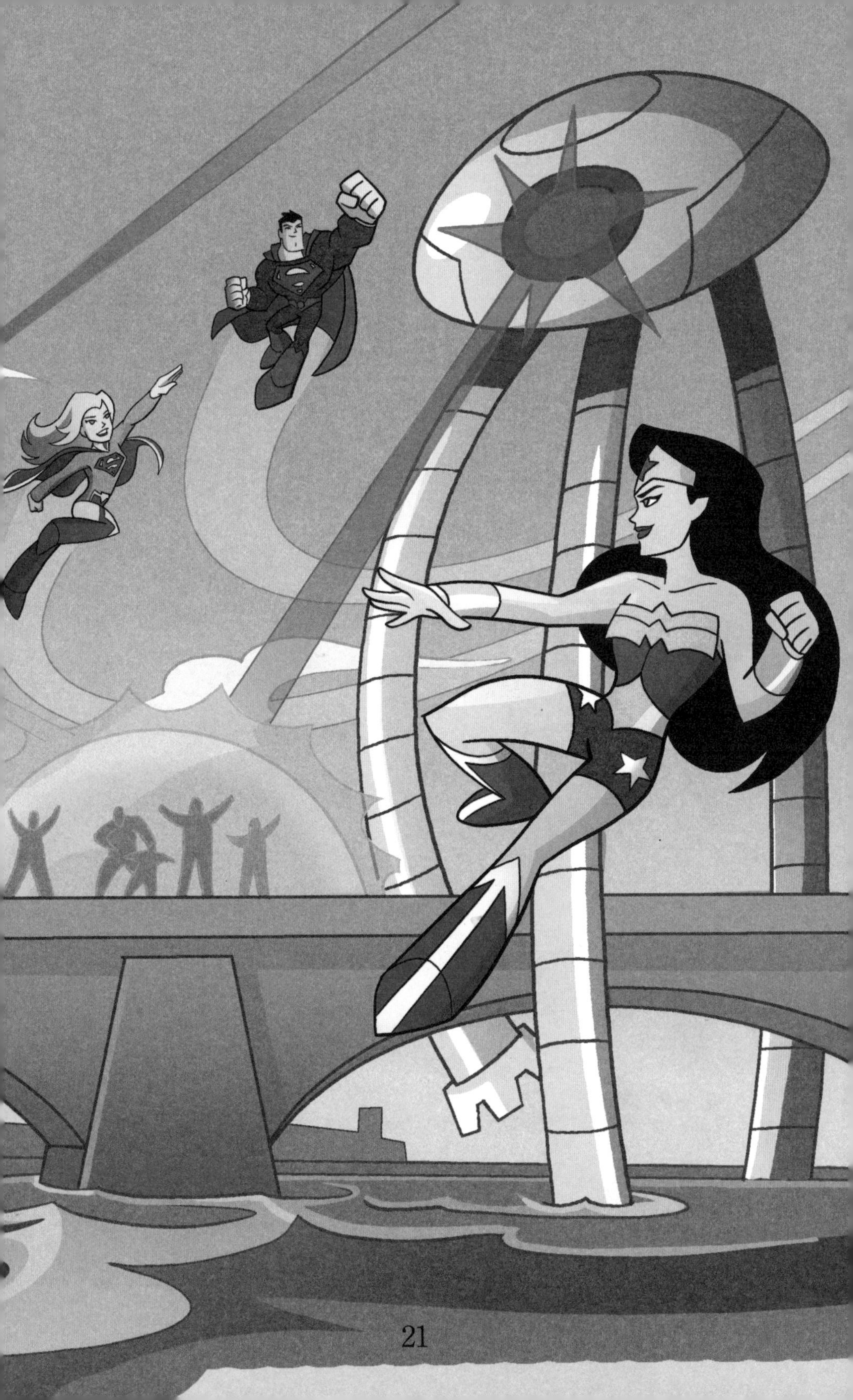

The Super Friends
work together to
defend their city.

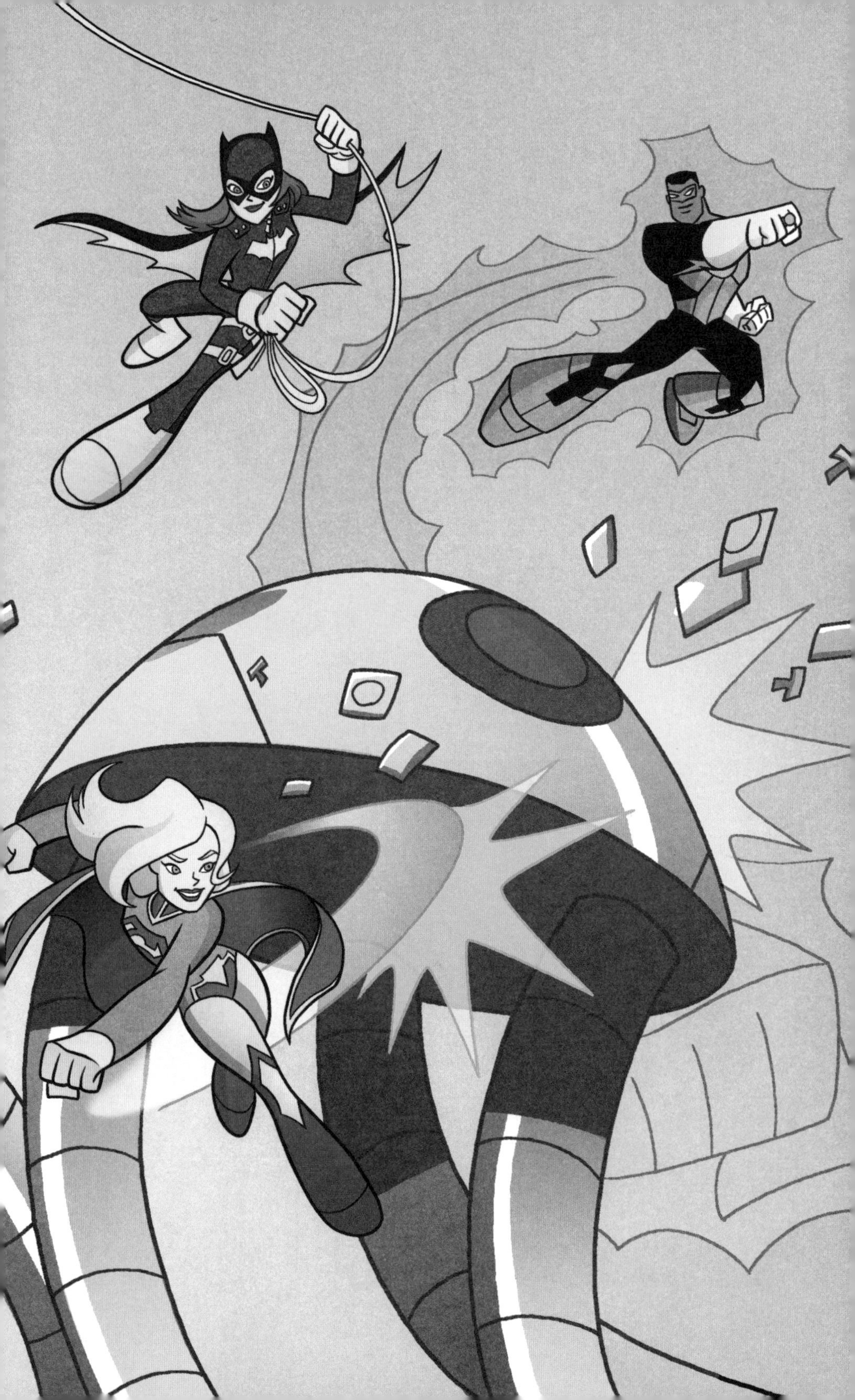

Wonder Woman
to the rescue!